Walt Disney

FAIRY TALE
TREASURY

Contents

Twin Books

GALLERY BOOKS
An imprint of W.H. Smith Publishers Inc.
112 Madison Avenue
New York, New York 10016

Published by Gallery Books
An Imprint of W H Smith Publishers Inc.
112 Madison Avenue
New York, New York 10016 USA

Produced by Twin Books
15 Sherwood Place
Greenwich, CT 06830 USA

ISBN 0-8317-9291-4

Printed in Hong Kong

1 2 3 4 5 6 7 8 9 10

(WALT DISNEY)

The Brave Little Tailor

Once upon a time, on a bright summer day, a little tailor sat working in his shop. A few tucks here, a button there, and his work would be done. Suddenly, he heard shouts outside his window.

The tailor looked up. *What's going on there?* he wondered.

"Hurry! Come and see the giant!" someone shouted. "The life-size picture of the giant in the town square. Come see how horrible he is!"

Horrible, is he? thought the little tailor. *No more horrible than these pesky flies!*

3

"Come on, shoo! Get away from me!"
The little tailor waved his arms madly, but the flies only attacked him more, and their buzzing seemed to grow louder.
Frustrated, the little tailor set his sewing aside and armed himself with two fly swatters. He brandished them menacingly.

"Come here, you little monsters!" he said.

A fierce battle began. The little tailor waved his weapons, beating back the flies. But every time he beat them back, they returned and attacked in full force until *splat*—he clapped the fly swatters against each other.

"Ha! Got you!" cried the little tailor. "Seven of them—with just one blow! Hurray!" Thrilled, the little tailor ran to the window.

"Hey, everyone! I killed seven with one blow!" Seven what, the little tailor didn't say. But seven was a lot!

The passersby couldn't believe their ears. A crowd gathered and the people nudged one another. Everyone wanted to know what all the excitement was about.

"Seven! Can you imagine!?" said someone in the crowd.

"Yes, with one blow!" said the little tailor, telling everyone proudly of his battle with the awful monsters. "They were everywhere!" he told them. "To my right! To my left! Above me!"

"Why, they must have been enormous!" said the baker. And so the flies had seemed to the little tailor. But none of them was as big as the tale that soon spread through the city.

"The little tailor slew seven giants, just like the one who is terrorizing the countryside!" someone finally told the castle guard.

"I must tell the king!" said the guard, and he raced up to the king's chamber.

The next day, the little tailor was summoned to the castle and taken before the king. "If you capture the giant," the king told him, "I will give you my daughter's hand in marriage."

"Capture the giant? Why that's…" The little tailor was about to say that capturing the giant was impossible. But one look into the starry eyes of the princess, and he knew he would have to try.

The townspeople formed a parade, and followed the little tailor to the city gates. "Thank you, my friends!" he called out, feeling especially proud and confident.

When he reached the edge of town, the gates quickly closed behind him. He turned for one last look at his beloved princess. As long as she was looking at him with those stars in her eyes, the little tailor knew he could take care of anything—even a giant.

But all too soon, the poor little tailor realized what he'd gotten himself into. He would have to fight the horrible giant all by himself—and he didn't have a chance! He sat on a rock, holding his head in his hands, heavy-hearted.

Everything had happened so fast! He'd hardly had time to think. If only he hadn't bragged about killing seven with one blow! He had only killed seven little flies, not seven giants, as everyone thought. But now, if he wanted to win the hand of the princess—and he did—and if he wanted to face his countrymen again, he had to capture that giant, no matter what!

All of a sudden, the little tailor saw something coming towards him. It was the towering giant! He was so tall, his head brushed the clouds. In a few seconds, the giant leaped across the river, stepped over a hill and crushed a farm. *Boom! Boom!* His footsteps shook the ground.

The little tailor gulped. "And they want *me* to take *him* prisoner? Impossible!" the little tailor said under his breath. He began to look around for a place to hide.

The little tailor decided he would have to say good-bye to his dreams of glory—and of marrying the princess. If he didn't get away soon, he would surely be flattened on the ground like a pancake. *And then what would the king think?* he wondered.

"Help!" he tried to cry out. Luckily, the cry stuck in his throat, and he remained unnoticed. Bending as low to the ground as possible, the little tailor tried to sneak away.

"Arghhhh!" roared the giant, and the sky above the little tailor disappeared. The giant's foot was a dark shape just above him.

The little tailor ran, trying to get out of the giant's path, but his short legs couldn't carry him far enough, fast enough. He looked around and saw a cart full of pumpkins. Quickly, he hopped into the cart and ducked down.

As the little tailor watched, the giant's foot crashed down on the ground like a clap of thunder.

Crack! A terrible noise ripped through the air. The giant had plopped down on top of a large house and crushed the roof. Fortunately, the people who lived in the house had already fled.

The poor little tailor had never felt so alone. *What should I do?* he wondered from his hiding place.

Then he saw the giant staring at the pumpkins, greedily licking his lips. "Oh, no!" gasped the little tailor in horror.

"Mmm...hungry!" grumbled the giant, rubbing his tummy. He grabbed a handful of pumpkins and tossed them into his gaping mouth.

The little tailor flattened himself against the bottom of the cart, hoping to escape the giant's notice.

"No!" screamed the little tailor. But he was already in the giant's hand. One quick toss in the air, and he was on his way into the huge open mouth. The giant's big teeth gleamed white in the sunlight.

Panicking, the little tailor waved his arms madly, looking for something to grab. Then he saw it—the giant's moustache. He quickly grabbed a handful of whiskers and held on for dear life. Then he hoisted himself all the way up onto the giant's nose.

"Uh…hey! What is that?" The giant made his eyes cross, trying to see what was tickling him. He reached up to grab what he thought was a little fly, but it slid down to his chest, then ran up his sleeve.

Quickly, the little tailor whipped out his scissors, cut through the shirt, and climbed out onto the giant's shoulder. Then he brandished his weapons—a needle and thread.

"Yoo-hoo!" the little tailor called up to the giant. "Try and catch me, you big ox!"

The giant slid his hand up his sleeve, but too late! The little tailor was sewing away furiously.

"Silk thread!" cried the little tailor, laughing. "It's unbreakable!" And there stood the giant, trapped with his arms crossed. So the little tailor plunged his needle in the fabric and finished his work, darting from the giant's left side to his right.

"Miserable little fly," snarled the giant. But there was nothing he could do! Soon he was tied up like a sausage.

The whole country came to congratulate the tailor on his victory. The king proclaimed a holiday. The giant slept, tied down securely.

And as the brave little tailor looked at his princess, he smiled tenderly. He had killed seven flies with one blow, and captured a giant singlehandedly with silken thread. He was a hero, after all.

Puss in Boots

Once upon a time, a poor miller died, leaving all he owned to his three sons. The oldest inherited the mill, the second son got the donkey, and the youngest got only the cat.

What rotten luck! thought the youngest son. *Both my brothers can earn a living, but how am I supposed to make any money from this cat?*

As if the cat could read his master's mind, he grinned and said, "Sir, if you give me a bag and a pair of boots, you'll see I can help you!"

"I might as well," the young man said. "I don't have much to lose. Here are the bag and boots that you ask for. Let's see what you can do!"

The cat pulled on the boots and dashed into the field, where he held the bag open in order to capture an unsuspecting rabbit. It wasn't long before one jumped right in.

Satisfied with his catch, Puss in Boots hurried to the king's palace. He bowed low before the throne. "Your Majesty," said the cat, "I have brought you this rabbit as a gift from my master, the Marquis of Carabas." (Puss in Boots felt very clever, making up this fine title for his poor master.)

"Thank the marquis for me!" said the king, extremely pleased with the gift.

Puss in Boots left the palace and headed for the fields again. This time, when he held his bag open, two fat partridges ventured into the trap. The cat tied the bag securely and marched back to the king. Again, His Majesty was delighted to receive such a gracious gift from the Marquis of Carabas, and he gave Puss in Boots some gold for his trouble.

For some days, Puss in Boots continued in this manner, until he overheard the king making plans for an outing with his daughter, the most beautiful princess in the world.

Puss in Boots hurried to find his master. The cat told him, "If you do as I say, you'll be rich and happy for the rest of your life. Simply bathe in the river where I show you. And from now on, if anyone asks, you are the Marquis of Carabas. Leave everything else to me."

The miller's son nodded obediently, and although he wasn't very happy about wading into the cold water, he did as he was told.

On the riverbank, Puss in Boots waited for the king's carriage.

"Help! Help!" the cat shouted when he saw the carriage. "My master, the Marquis of Carabas, is drowning!"

The king leaned his head out the carriage window and recognized the cat who had brought him all the delicious game.

"Quick! Save the Marquis of Carabas!" the king ordered.

While his master was being fished out of the river, Puss in Boots hid the young man's clothes under a rock. Then he scampered back to the carriage.

"Your Majesty," the cat exclaimed, "thieves have stolen my master's clothes! He has nothing to wear!"

When the king heard this, he commanded, "Knights of the Wardrobe, fetch my finest garments to clothe the honorable Marquis of Carabas!"

Swifter than lightning, the king's attendants returned with the royal garments. The miller's son looked very handsome in his new clothes, and the king's daughter found him quite charming. It was obvious to everyone that the beautiful princess was falling in love.

Without hesitating, the king asked, "Won't you join us in the carriage, my dear Marquis?"

Puss in Boots was delighted with the way his plan was working. He ran ahead of the carriage to a meadow where some peasants were working. "Good men," the cat cried, "if you don't tell the king that this meadow belongs to the Marquis of Carabas, you'll never be heard from again!"

The cat ran farther on, and he found some men who were harvesting wheat. "Good people," he called, "if you don't tell the king that these fields belong to the Marquis of Carabas, you'll never be heard from again!"

Sure enough, when the king came upon the wheat harvesters, he asked, "My fine fellows, who owns these fields?"

"The Marquis of Carabas, Sire!" cried the men, remembering the cat's threat.

The king smiled, thinking, "This marquis must be very rich!"

As the carriage rolled through the countryside, Puss in Boots went on ahead. Soon he came to a magnificent castle.

"Who owns this castle?, he asked a peasant.

"An ogre owns it," said the man. "He also owns all the land that surrounds it."

From the peasant, Puss in Boots found out all he could about the ogre, then marched up and knocked on the castle door.

"I wish to pay my respects to the castle's owner," he said to the servant who answered the door.

The cat was ushered inside. With his boot heels clicking loudly
on the stone floor, he strode down the long hall until he reached
the room where the ogre was dining.

Puss in Boots bowed deeply.

"Excuse me, Sire, for interrupting your supper," said the daring cat, "but is it true that you have the power to transform yourself into any creature...such as a large fearsome beast?"

"Indeed!" snarled the ogre, and he turned into a huge angry lion.

When the lion took a swipe at him, Puss in Boots jumped!

As soon as the ogre became himself again, the cunning cat began to tease him. "Although I find it difficult to believe," he said, "I have also been told that you can change yourself into a very small creature, like a rat or a mouse. Could this be possible?"

The moment the ogre turned into a mouse, Puss in Boots caught him and gobbled him up!

Now that the ogre was gone, the splendid castle and the rich lands surrounding it needed a new owner. And Puss in Boots knew just who that would be!

The cat also knew that the king's carriage would pass by the castle at any moment. He ordered the cooks to prepare a feast, then ran outside to flag down the royal coach.

Puss in Boots need not have worried. When the king saw the castle from the road, he was eager to meet the owner of such a beautiful place. He commanded his driver to cross the drawbridge.

"Welcome, Your Majesty, to the castle of my honorable master, the Lord Marquis of Carabas!" cried Puss in Boots with a low bow.

"The marquis must be even richer than I thought!" exclaimed the king. "This castle is almost as fine as my own!"

Behind him, the miller's son and the princess were gazing into each other's eyes.

Puss in Boots showed the king into the dining hall, where the banquet had been laid out.

Reassured by the wealth of the marquis, and seeing that his daughter had never been happier, the king raised his glass in a toast. "It is up to you, my dear marquis," he said. "Do you wish to be my son-in-law?"

So the fortunate Marquis of Carabas and the most beautiful princess in the world were wed that night in the castle's chapel.

As for Puss in Boots, he was made a lord, and never again had to chase mice...except for his own amusement!

The Princess and the Pea

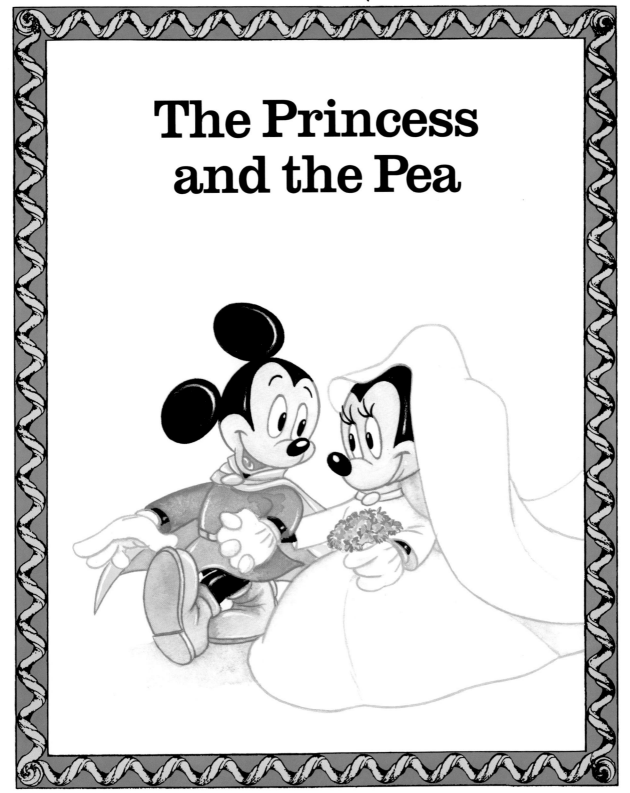

Once upon a time there was a handsome young prince, who was determined to marry only a real princess. His mother introduced him to all the princesses she could think of, but he didn't like any of them.

"I guess I'll have to find the right princess on my own," he said to himself. And off he rode to find her.

The prince went to every castle he could think of, and met all kinds of princesses, but none of them was the right one.

One was too old, another was too thin, yet another was too tall.

Alas, poor prince! Where would he find his dream princess?

The prince spent a whole year looking for a real princess. He left castle after castle without finding one to marry. Tired and discouraged, he decided to head for home. The leaves had all fallen, and the wind had turned cold. Soon it would be winter, and no time to be out on the road looking for princesses.

His mother and father were glad to welcome him home, but sad that his long search had been in vain.

One night, soon after the prince had returned, a terrible storm blew up. The wind howled, and driving rain clattered against the castle roof. Thunder crashed, and lightning flashed through angry grey clouds. The storm raged against the castle, making those inside thankful for its sturdy stone walls.

The prince and his parents huddled close to the fireplace in the great hall. "I hope all of my subjects have the sense to stay in out of this weather," said the king.

Even as he spoke, a bedraggled figure was scurrying across the moat to find shelter.

Suddenly, there was a loud knocking at the door. The king could hardly believe his ears! Who could survive outdoors in this storm?

The knocking became a hammering. "Please open the door!" came the plaintive cry over the shrieking of the wind.

The king jumped up and rushed to the door and drew back the heavy iron bolt.

The king could hardly believe his eyes! At the door was a young woman who looked like a very soggy princess.

Remembering his duties as host, the king stopped staring and motioned to the young woman. "Come in! Come in, poor child," he said. "Go sit by the fire! I'll attend to your servants."

He looked outside, but the young woman was alone and on foot—no carriage, no attendants—rather odd, for a princess.

Once the princess had dried out by the fire, they sat down to a nice, hot meal. The queen noticed that the prince couldn't keep his eyes off the stranger. After dinner, as the king led the princess back to the fire, the queen asked her son what he thought of this princess.

"I think I would like to marry her," replied the prince. "But I must be sure she's a real princess."

"I think I know how to find out," said his mother. "Leave it to me."

The queen ordered the servants to follow her to one of the
guest rooms, bringing all the spare mattresses in the castle. She
placed a single dried pea on the bed, then told the servants to
bring in all the mattresses they had found. These spare mattresses
were all the finest quality. No one who had slept on one of them
had ever had the slightest complaint.

The queen ordered the servants to pile up all the mattresses on top of the dried pea. The result looked a little odd. All those mattresses made a very high bed, but an extremely well-cushioned one.

"Perfect!" said the queen to herself. Her scheme was foolproof. Anyone but a true princess would sleep like a baby on top of all those excellent mattresses.

Meanwhile, the princess was getting more and more drowsy as she sat in front of the fire, trying to pay attention to the prince's questions, and to answer properly in the right places. When the queen returned, she excused herself and the princess and took her guest up to bed.

"I've had this cozy bed made up especially for you," said the queen, "so you will be sure to sleep well after all you've been through."

The princess had never seen, much less slept in, such a high bed! "Good night," said the queen. "Sleep tight."

The princess put on the nightdress and cap that had been laid out for her and climbed up the ladder, all the way to the top mattress. She slipped under the soft comforter and settled down to sleep.

"At last!" she thought to herself, snuggling down on the feather pillow.

Suddenly, her eyes popped open. For some reason, she couldn't get comfortable!

She wriggled around on the bed, trying to find a soft spot. She tried closing her eyes again; again they popped open. All night long she tried to get to sleep. All night long, she stayed awake. Poor princess!

The next morning, when the queen went to wake the princess, she found a very droopy young woman.

"My dear! You look so...tired," observed the queen. "Didn't you sleep well?"

"I don't want to offend you, Your Majesty," the princess replied, "but I didn't sleep a wink. No matter how I tried to get comfortable, it felt as if I were sleeping on a rock."

Overjoyed that she had at last found a true princess, the queen grabbed the young woman's hand and ran down to tell her son. She was just in time. He was in the courtyard, his horse saddled, ready to set out yet again on his search for a bride.

When he heard the news, he was thrilled. He grabbed the princess's hand, kissed it, and asked her to marry him.

Just then, there was a commotion outside the castle walls. Into the courtyard clattered a fine coach, pulled by four white horses and accompanied by attendants in satin uniforms.

"We're so glad we found you, Your Highness!" the coachman said to the princess. "Let us continue our journey home."

The princess and the prince bid a fond farewell. He arranged to travel to her castle, to ask her father for her hand in marriage.

Of course, the princess's father approved of the match. The prince was, after all, a very nice prince, and he convinced the princess's father that he would be a good husband.

On the day of the wedding, all the people in both kingdoms celebrated. The ceremony in which the prince and princess pledged their love to one another was very touching (both queens cried), the wedding feast was delicious, and the dancing went on until morning.

All their subjects cheered when the prince brought his princess home to his castle. The people had all heard about the pea under the mattresses, and were very proud of the fact that the prince's bride was a true princess.

The prince and princess set up their household in the roomy old castle, and before long the ancient walls once again rang with the joyful cries of children. No one was happier with this state of affairs than the king and queen.

All the little princes and princesses were the apples of their parents' eyes—and of their grandparents' eyes, too. The king could never get enough of playing "horsie," and the queen could always be counted on to rock the cradle. You could say they all lived happily ever after!

Little Red Riding Hood

Once upon a time, there lived a sweet young girl known as Little Red Riding Hood. She got her name from the red hooded cloak that her grandmother had made for her. The little girl liked it so much that she wore it every day.

Little Red Riding Hood lived with her mother in a cottage in the forest. One day her mother said, "Grandmother isn't feeling well, dear. Please take her this basket filled with goodies. But don't dawdle on the way! Go straight to grandmother's house without stopping."

"I promise, Mother!" said Little Red Riding Hood.

The little girl took the basket and went skipping into the forest. As she made her way down the sunlit path, the birds and forest creatures came out to greet her. "Good morning, Little Red Riding Hood! Good morning!" they chattered.

"Hello, rabbit! Hello, squirrel!" she called back.

Although her grandmother lived far away on the other side of the forest, Little Red Riding Hood wasn't at all afraid of the long journey ahead of her. When she saw some beautiful wildflowers growing beside the path, she said to herself, "Surely Mother wouldn't mind if I stopped to pick a daisy or two!"

Little Red Riding Hood set down her basket. "I have plenty of time to gather a bouquet for Grandma," she said to herself. "She'll be so pleased with the pretty flowers that she'll feel better in no time!"

As the little girl reached for a daffodil, the forest-dwellers whispered, "Run away, Little Red Riding Hood! The Big Bad Wolf is coming!" But the little girl didn't hear them. She was too busy gathering flowers.

"Hello, Little Red Riding Hood!" said the wolf. "Where are you going on this lovely morning with such a big basket of food?"

"I'm going to see my grandmother. She isn't feeling very well," replied Little Red Riding Hood, trembling as she spoke. "My mother told me to go straight to Grandma's house without stopping."

"Does your grandmother live very far from here?" the wolf asked, smiling sweetly.

"On the other side of the forest, by the mill," answered Little Red Riding Hood.

"Your grandmother and I are good friends," said the wolf. "I'll go see her, too. Why don't you take one path, and I'll take the other...and we'll see who gets there first!" Without another word, the wolf dashed into the forest.

Little Red Riding Hood felt much better after the wolf had gone. She didn't really believe that he was going to see her grandmother, so she picked some more flowers before continuing on her way.

While Little Red Riding Hood was strolling along, the Big Bad Wolf was racing through the forest. He knew a short cut that would take him to the grandmother's house in half the time it would take Little Red Riding Hood to get there—even if she didn't dawdle.

What a silly little girl she is, thought the wolf as he hurried along. *But she'll make a tasty supper, silly or not. What a nice surprise for me!*

It wasn't long before the wolf reached the grandmother's cottage. He knocked on the door and called, "It's Little Red Riding Hood, Grandmother—and I've brought some goodies for you to eat!" The wolf spoke in such a sweet voice that he sounded just like the little girl.

Grandma was awakened from a sound sleep by the knocking. She reached for her spectacles and sat up in bed. "The door is open," she called. "Come in, my dear."

The wolf did as he was told.

He pushed open the door...and bounded into the cottage.
Because Grandma was expecting to see Little Red Riding Hood,
the Big Bad Wolf gave her quite a shock!

She leaped out of bed, screaming, "Get out! Get out of my house, you Big Bad Wolf!"

But the wolf simply ignored her. He had a plan, and he intended to follow it.

He strode toward the grandmother until she backed into the closet. "I'm not going to eat you now," he snarled. "I'll just lock you in here. Then I'll borrow a nightdress and a cap, and when Little Red Riding Hood arrives, I'll be the one who answers the door. I'll make a great granny, just wait and see!"

There was no way for the poor grandmother to escape.

When the wolf had tied Grandma up and locked her in the closet, he plucked off his hat and put on the nightdress and cap. He looked in the mirror and admired his disguise.

As he was waiting for Little Red Riding Hood, he sang this song:

Red Riding Hood will soon appear
With goodies for her granny dear,
And never know it's me *that's here!*

The wolf stopped singing when he heard a knock at the door.

The wolf jumped into bed and pulled the covers up to his eyes. He coughed, then said in his sweetest voice, "Who's there?"

"It's Little Red Riding Hood, Grandma. I've brought some goodies for you to eat!"

"Lift the latch, and come in!" called the wolf.

When Little Red Riding Hood entered the cottage, the wolf said, "Put down your basket and come closer, dear!"

The little girl approached the bed. "My, what big ears you have, Grandma!" she said.

The wolf replied, "The better to hear you with, my child!"
"Goodness, Grandma, what big eyes you have!" added the girl.
"All the better to see you with, my dear!" said the wolf.
"And oh, Grandma, what big teeth you have!"
"All the better to eat you with!" growled the wolf, and he jumped out of bed, ready to gobble her up!

Little Red Riding Hood sprang to the window and threw it open. "Help!" she shouted, as loudly as she could. "The Big Bad Wolf is after me!"

Fortunately, a hunter was passing by at that very moment. He whirled around and ran to the cottage.

The hunter rushed to the window. He raised his gun and fired
at the Big Bad Wolf.

The wolf yelped and sprinted out the door. Even though he
hadn't been hit, he felt as if his tail were on fire!

The Big Bad Wolf disappeared into the forest.
As Little Red Riding Hood watched him run away, she knew she had made a big mistake, dawdling in the forest and speaking to a stranger.

The hunter let the grandmother out of the closet, and the old woman hugged Little Red Riding Hood. Then she said to the hunter, "Thank you, sir, for saving me and my granddaughter. And I must say, I suddenly feel much better!"

All three of them decided to go on a picnic. While they were enjoying the food from Little Red Riding Hood's basket, they told the story of the Big Bad Wolf over and over again.

Little Red Riding Hood admitted her mistake. Grandmother described how frightened she had been and showed them the hat that the wolf left behind. And the hunter described in detail everything that had happened while Grandmother was locked in the closet. Although he was quite proud of himself for scaring off the wolf, Little Red Riding Hood and her grandmother didn't mind hearing his tale at all. Where would they have been without him?